Maury Had a Little Lamb

Janette Oke's Animal Friends

JANETTE OKE'S

Animal Friends

Maury Had a Little Lamb

Illustrated by Nancy Munger

BETHANY BACKYARD®

Maury Had a Little Lamb
Revised, full-color edition 2001
Copyright © 1989, 2001
Janette Oke
Illustrations by Nancy Munger
Design by Jennifer Parker

Library of Congress Cataloging-in-Publication Data

Oke, Janette, 1935-
  Maury had a little lamb / by Janette Oke ; illustrated by Nancy
Munger.— Rev., full-color ed.
      p. cm. — (Janette Oke's animal friends)
Summary: Shandy the lamb, rejected by his mother and the other
ewes, is cared for by a young boy until he is big enough to try to
rejoin the flock of sheep.
  ISBN 0-7642-2457-3 (pbk.)
  [1. Sheep—Fiction. 2. Animals—Infancy—Fiction. 3. Farm
life—Fiction. 4. Orphans—Fiction.] I. Munger, Nancy, ill. II. Title.
  PZ7.O4144 Mau 2001
  [Fic]—dc21
                                    00-012203

Dedicated with our love
to Katherine Louise (Katie),
born December 18, 1988,
to Lorne and Debbie Oke
and to
Courtney Elizabeth,
baby sister for Ashley,
born February 23, 1989,
to Terry and Barbara Oke.
We, your grandparents,
and your cousins Nate and Jessica Logan,
welcome you to the family.

JANETTE OKE was born in Champion, Alberta, during the depression years, to a Canadian prairie farmer and his wife. She is a graduate of Mountain View Bible College in Didsbury, Alberta, where she met her husband, Edward. Both Janette and Edward have been active in their local church as Sunday school teachers and board members. The Okes have four grown children and several grandchildren and make their home near Calgary, Alberta.

CHAPTER
One

"What's going on?" I said to myself. It was dark and noisy, and I was hungry. Where was I?

Suddenly, warm hands were lifting me. The noises that I had heard began to change to voices.

"You poor little thing," someone was saying in my ear. "Poor little thing. Your mama doesn't want triplets. She's afraid if she tries to feed three, there won't be enough milk for everyone."

The hands were gentle as they stroked back and forth over my curly white coat. But the pain in my stomach was still there.

"We'll find you another mama," said

the voice, and then he called loudly, "Da-ad."

I heard an answer from somewhere in the distance. "Yes?"

"The ewe won't take her lamb."

I could hear footsteps coming. "But I checked her just a few minutes ago. I thought she had accepted them both."

"But she has three—*three*."

"Are you sure?" The deeper voice had almost reached us now.

"I'm sure. See?" And I was pushed toward a much bigger man.

He took me. His hands were much larger than the ones that had been holding me, but I wasn't scared. He was gentle.

"Well, I'll be!" he said as he moved forward to look in the pen. "Triplets."

"Isn't it cute, Daddy? But the mama won't feed it. What will we do? It has to eat."

"We'll find another ewe. One that has only one lamb. But it doesn't always work, Maury. Sometimes they don't accept an orphan."

"He's hungry," said Maury. "I saw him. I saw him try to get some dinner, but the other lambs and the mama wouldn't let him eat."

"He'll be hungry—that's for sure," agreed Maury's father.

"Let's hurry!" Maury exclaimed. "Let's find a new mama."

CHAPTER
Two

There was a lot of moving around then. Maury set me down next to lots of mother sheep. I was excited because it meant I would eat soon. But ewe after ewe turned her back on me, moved out of my reach, or butted me away. It seemed that nobody wanted a skinny, brand-new, half-starved lamb.

"What'll we do now, Dad?" asked Maury.

"Guess there's only one thing to do. We'll have to bottle-feed him."

"Bottle-feed?"

"Caring for a newborn lamb takes a great deal of time and attention. It's a big job, Maury. You'll need to help him eat and make sure he's taken care of all day long. Are you interested?"

I felt myself lifted eagerly from the larger hands to smaller ones. The boy named Maury cuddled me close. He put one hand under my chin so that he could look at my face.

"Sure," he said. I could hear the excitement in his voice.

"Come on, then," said the father. "He's waited too long already. We'd better get some milk in that empty tummy."

It sure did sound good to me. It seemed to take forever for them to get my bottle ready. But finally they were pushing something toward me. I could smell milk.

At first I was a bit messy, but I was so hungry that I didn't care. I could feel the warm milk flowing down my throat and filling the big emptiness inside. My tail began to flick, back and forth, back and forth. It felt so good to be getting something to eat. And I knew that Maury was going to take extra special care of me.

CHAPTER
Three

"After he fed me, Maury introduced me to his sister, Jenny.

"Can I hold him? Can I hold him?" she begged.

"His tummy is full," warned Maury.

"I'll be careful. I'll hold still."

Maury's mother cut in. "I think you'd better let him sleep now. There'll be lots of time to hold him later. He needs to rest now if he is going to grow properly."

"Aww," Jenny whined.

"Tell you what," said Maury. "You can hold him while I fix him a bed. But you've got to hold him still. And don't press on his tummy."

"I will. I won't," promised Jenny.

Jenny settled me against her own small body and held me very carefully. Suddenly, I felt so tired. I couldn't even hold my eyes open. I just wanted to curl right up and go to sleep. But I couldn't curl up the way Jenny was holding me.

"Now, you remember," I heard the mama saying. "He's only to be in the house for a little while. He'll have to go out with the other sheep just as soon as he doesn't need to eat quite as often."

"I promise," agreed Maury.

"And I don't want you coaxing to keep him here longer than is necessary."

"I won't," Maury promised.

I didn't know what all of the fuss was about. It was true that the house had some rather strange odors. It didn't smell nearly as nice as the warm, sweet straw—but I really didn't mind. I'd manage somehow.

I was lifted from Jenny's arms and placed into a nice, cozy box. The bottom was soft and snuggly. I was hoping that Maury would join me so that we could cuddle up together, but he didn't.

I felt very lonely. I bleated, and a hand reached in to stroke my woolly back. I felt a bit better then.

"Lie down," coaxed Maury. "Just lie down. You need to rest. You'll be warm here."

He gently eased me down on the soft-ness. I was so tired I couldn't even protest. I curled myself into a ball, tucked my chin against my body, and let my eyes close.

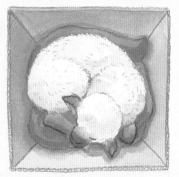

It felt so good

just to relax. It felt so good to have a full tummy! It felt so good to have a hand stroking my back. I decided that I was going to like my new friend Maury.

C H A P T E R
Four

"He needs a name." It was Jenny's voice that reached me. "We can't just call him 'Lamb' all the time."

"I've been thinking about it," said Maury.

"I think we should call him Snowflake," continued Jenny.

"Naw."

"I know," called Jenny, bouncing around. "Tiny."

But Maury just frowned and shook his head.

"Well, he is tiny," said Jenny defiantly, shaking her curls.

"He won't always be tiny," Maury was

21

quick to respond. "Dad says that the way he eats, he'll be big in no time."

Maury put me back to bed and left the room. I didn't sleep very long. When I woke up it wasn't because I was hungry. I was just tired of being tired, I guess. My legs felt funny. Like they needed to stretch—or jump—or something.

Maury must have heard me stirring about. He came into the room.

"What's the matter, Lamb?" he asked me, bending to scratch my ear. "You can't be hungry already."

"Maybe he needs some exercise," Maury's mother suggested. "It's a nice day. Why don't you take him out and let him run around the yard for a while?"

Maury lifted me and started from the room. As he walked toward the door, he grabbed a light jacket from a hook and wiggled his way into it.

"It's a little cold," he informed me. "It's still early spring, you know."

When we got to the yard, Maury set me down. He was right. It felt cold.

"Come on," he coaxed. "Run around a little."

He started to move away from me, and I panicked at the thought of being alone. "Baa," I cried and ran after him.

Maury began to laugh. I guess he thought that I sounded funny.

"C'mon," he called. "Run faster."

I was surprised at how much better my legs were working. Why, yesterday I could barely stand, and here I was chasing after Maury.

Maury was laughing now. "C'mon," he called again.

I followed after him, round and round

the yard. I soon realized that we were playing some kind of game. I liked it. My legs
liked it. It made them feel much better to
stretch a bit.

I even tried a couple jumps just to see if
they would work. They did. I jumped again,
twisting sideways in the air before I came
down. Maury laughed.

I ran over to the fence to try jumping
again, when suddenly a great big animal
poked out a nose and then came right
toward me. I stopped dead in my tracks. My
mind said that I should run for Maury, but
my legs refused to take a step.

The big thing came nearer and nearer. I
just stood there shaking and shivering in
fear. I was sure that it was going to eat me
right up!

CHAPTER
Five

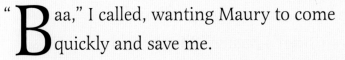

"Baa," I called, wanting Maury to come quickly and save me.

The big animal reached out a long nose. Then he took a lick. I was sure that he was just sampling, to see if he really wanted to eat me or not. I could see many sharp teeth in his mouth as he ran his tongue over his lips.

"Baa," I said again.

And then, as if by some miracle, Maury was at my side. But he didn't scoop me up quickly and run as I had hoped he would. Instead, he plopped himself down on the ground beside me.

"I've got a new lamb, Buster," Maury

said, reaching out a hand to stroke the big animal. "Isn't he cute?"

I guess the big animal, Buster, wasn't too impressed. He turned his back on both of us and walked slowly back to his house in the corner. I was very relieved.

"That's Buster," Maury told me. "He's our sheep dog. He's really good with sheep. We have two dogs. Buster and Babs."

Maury did pick me up then. I was still shivering.

"Hey, Lamb, you're cold," said Maury. "I'd better get you in."

There was no way that I could tell Maury that I'd just been scared half out of my wits.

"Mom," said Maury as we entered the house. "Would you help me?"

His mother looked up from the book she was holding.

"I need a name for my lamb."

"What kind of name are you thinking of?" his mother asked.

"Well, I don't want Snow. And I don't want Tiny or Peewee or anything like that," Maury informed her.

She seemed to think about that. "Maybe we can find a name in the name book. It's on the fireplace bookshelf."

Maury ran and was soon back with a book in his hand. I sat between them, eager to hear what they would pick.

"Sean, Seldon, Seth, Seymour," she read. But with each name Maury shook his head.

"Shalom. Shamus. Shandy. Oh, look at this. Shandy means rambunctious."

"What's rambunctious?" asked Maury.

"That's almost like frisky," said his mother.

"It is?" Maury's eyes were big. He was thinking about the name. "Shandy," he said. "Shandy. I like it. It's different. And it suits him." He began to grin. "Yeah, I think I'll call him Shandy. Thanks, Mom."

Maury scooped me up and moved me off to the kitchen.

"Shandy," he said. I didn't know if he was talking to me or himself. "I like it. Do you like it? I think it suits you."

"Baa," I said in reply. I did like it. But I was hungry again, and I was much more interested in some food than in my name.

CHAPTER
Six

A few mornings later, a strange thing happened. Maury and Jenny both seemed to be rushing madly about the house. Maury had given me my breakfast, but I could tell he was in a hurry. He kept urging me to finish my bottle quickly.

As soon as I had swallowed the last drop, he placed me back in my box and almost ran from the room. I could hear the family in the kitchen.

"Well," said the father. "Your little break is over. It's back to school again for you."

"What are you going to do about Shandy?" Jenny asked around a mouthful of

31

something.

"Mom's gonna feed him" came the reply from Maury.

"Bet he'll be lonesome," continued Jenny.

"I'll only be gone about six and a half hours," answered Maury.

I didn't understand anything about hours, but Maury seemed to feel that it wouldn't be too long until he'd be home again.

"He'll still be lonesome."

"I can't help it," said Maury. "I have to go to school."

"You certainly do," replied his mother. "Don't worry. I've fed many a lamb in my day. Shandy and I will get along just fine."

"I wasn't really worried about his bottle," said Maury. "I... I was just thinkin' that he might miss me."

"Oh, he will. But he'll be fine," his
mother promised. "Now, you'd better hurry
or you'll miss the bus."

Soon Maury was kneeling beside my
box. His hand ran over my back and then
stroked my head.

"Sorry, Shandy," he said. His voice
sounded sad. "Sorry. Our break is over. I
have to go back to school today."

Maury was gone then, and I was alone
in the room. I heard the door slam, and
then the house was quiet.

CHAPTER
Seven

I thought that I was all alone until I heard noises in the kitchen. The mother was still with me. I called to her, but she didn't answer. I called again.

The door opened and she came into the room.

"What's the matter with you?" she asked me. "You've just been fed."

I wanted out. I wanted to be held. I wanted to follow her back to the kitchen.

"Baa," I said again.

"I have work to do," she told me. "You just settle down there and have a nap."

At last I gave up. I curled into a ball and tried to sleep.

It was a long time before I was able to drop off, but I didn't sleep for long. I stood to my feet and started calling again. The house was awfully quiet. I was afraid that there was no one home.

"Baa," I called as loudly as I could.

She came in then, wiping her hands on her apron. Under her arm was tucked my bottle.

"So you want to eat again? Well, here you are." She knelt down beside the box.

She didn't lift me from the box and hold me as Maury always did. Instead, she held the bottle out to me and laughed as I ate.

"My, you are hungry. No wonder you are growing so quickly. Just look at you."

I gave a little bunt with my head and began to drink even faster.

"Hey, slow down," she chuckled. "You

don't need to be in such a hurry. I'm not going to take it away until you're all finished."

True to her word, she waited right there until I had completely drained the bottle. I thought that she would pick me up and hold me then, but she didn't.

"There you go," she said and stroked my back. "You should feel just fine now."

I didn't feel fine. I just felt full. I still felt lonesome. I tried to tell her so.

"Now, lie back down and have another nap," she told me. "Before you know it, Maury will be home, and then he'll take you for a little run."

But the day seemed to drag on and on, and Maury didn't come. I couldn't sleep. I was much too lonesome. I was fed again, but I wasn't held that time, either. I wanted Maury. Would he never return?

I had decided that something terrible had happened and Maury wouldn't be coming back, when I heard the door bang. Maury hurried into the room, scattering his lunch pail, books, and jacket behind him.

"Shandy!" he called. "Shandy—I'm home."

Oh, I was glad to see him! He scooped me up and held me close, stroking my sides and telling me how much he had missed me. I wanted to tell him that I had missed him, too. But I didn't know how to say it. I was just so glad that the long day was finally over.

CHAPTER
Eight

I thought school was just for one day. So imagine my sadness the next morning when it happened again. Maury and Jenny rushed all around, and then they were off to school.

I was heartbroken. I thought we were all through with that. But morning after morning it was the same. Hurry, hurry, hurry, and then off to the school bus while I complained all alone.

I was fed well, and I wasn't cold. My box was always clean. I had nice, soft bedding. But I was lonesome and unhappy until I heard the slam of the door and knew that Maury was home.

And then one day things turned from bad to worse.

"Maury, I think it's time for Shandy to be moved out of the house," his mother announced.

"Aww," began Maury, but he was quickly stopped.

"Remember. No coaxing. You promised. The days are much warmer now. Look at him. He's getting too big for that box. He'll soon be jumping out. He almost did yesterday."

So she had noticed, I thought to myself. I thought she wasn't looking.

"But—" began Maury.

"No buts. He's perfectly big enough to be out in the barn with the other sheep. He doesn't need to eat nearly as often anymore."

"All right," Maury said.

Maury picked me up and carried me outside. Together we headed for the big barn across the yard.

"You're gonna live with the other sheep," he told me. "You won't be lonesome there."

We entered the barn, and Maury leaned over a fence and set me gently on the floor. I recognized the smell. It was the nice-smelling straw again.

"There you go," he said. "Go make some friends." He nudged me forward gently.

I hesitated. I wasn't sure what I should do.

Just as I was about to move forward, a big ewe came toward me. Close at her heels was another ewe of the flock. They were just close enough to reach out and sniff at my coat.

I was just ready to bound forward excitedly, when the first ewe snorted and exclaimed, "What are you doing here? You're a stranger. I don't even know you. You don't belong in this pen."

"What?" said the other. "A stranger? How'd he get in here? Where are the dogs?"

I made the mistake of moving then. Just one little step forward, but it was one too many. The first ewe caught me solidly with the top of her head. The blow made me dizzy. I was just finding my feet when the

other ewe gave me another butt. I cried out, afraid for my life.

Then I felt hands lifting me. Maury was there. He had rescued me just in time.

"They don't want you," he said as he stroked me gently. "They think that you might hurt their lambs. Silly old sheep. You can't go in there. I'll tell Mom."

And talking and stroking, he took me back to the house.

CHAPTER
Nine

Maury decided that he and his father could build a special pen for me in the barn. It would still be with the other sheep. But I would be fenced in so they couldn't hurt me. I guess Maury hoped that in time they would accept me. I wasn't too sure.

Maury placed me in the pen and then climbed in with me. He reached out a hand to me, but he didn't pick me up.

"This is your new home, Shandy," he informed me. "See, it's big enough for you to run. It has straw on the floor, just like the other sheep. You'll like it here."

Back against the far wall, three ewes lay

close together, visiting with one another. Here and there lambs played or slept. It was interesting to watch the pen of sheep. For the first time, I felt very left out. And I felt terrified when I realized Maury was going to leave me here!

"There. There you are," Maury said softly. "Now, you curl right up here and go to sleep. I'll be back soon with your bottle. I need to do my other chores now. Here. Lie down. You won't be lonesome. You have all the other sheep."

Maury pushed me into my box and tried to get me to lie down. I resisted—my legs stiff so they wouldn't bend. He gave up.

"Well, stand up then if you want to. But

when you get tired, go to bed in here. I'll be back soon."

And with those words, Maury turned and closed the barn door behind him.

What will I do now? I wondered. *When will Maury come back?*

Just how long would I have to stay in this pen by myself before they decided what to do with me?

CHAPTER
Ten

Each day when Maury returned from school, he would come to the sheep barn and we'd spend some time playing together in the yard. The piles of snow were gone. In their place, green grass began to show.

I liked the grass much better. I found out that it tasted even better than it looked. It was juicy and sweet, and I couldn't seem to get enough of it. I wanted to share it with Maury, but he didn't seem one bit interested in trying it.

I still had my bottle. I would have been lost without it, but the green grass tasted good, too.

Day by day, other greens began to grow, too. I was sure that it would taste just as good as the grass, but every time I headed for it, I was shooed away by Maury.

"Stay out of Mom's flower beds," he'd scold. "Or she'll be really mad."

I went back to eating the grass again. But I did keep my eyes open just in case Maury got busy with something else. I got my chance a few weeks later.

"The carrots," Maury was mumbling. "Mom said to do the carrots."

Maury had taken me out of my pen so I could play while he did chores.

"Boy," he said, and he didn't sound happy. "Look at all the carrot seeds I have to plant!"

He stood shaking his head, and then he
dropped down on his knees and began to
pick at something. While he dug in the dirt,
I decided to have a look around.

Just a few feet away, and out of Maury's
sight, were rows of pots. And in each pot,
there were lots of different types of flowers.
They were so pretty and smelled so good, I
knew I'd have to take a nibble.

Maury was too busy to realize what I
was doing. On and on down the row he
went, digging and planting, digging and
planting. Suddenly, he stopped and looked
around. I stopped, too.

He sat there on his heels for a minute,
wiping the moisture from his brow. Then
after a moment or two, he went back to digging. I went right on eating.

We were almost at the end of the row
when Maury straightened and looked

around. He was still grumbling about the carrots as he stretched his back. He looked around the garden. I guess he was looking for me.

"Shandy," he called. "Shandy, where are you?"

I answered from right behind him.

He turned to look back at me, then he sprang to his feet, shouting, "Shandy! What have you done?"

CHAPTER
Eleven

"Mom is going to be angry," Maury said. "You'd better get outta here quick."

But it was already too late. We both heard his mother coming at just that moment.

"Oh boy!" groaned Maury.

"How're you doing?" Maury's mother called as she entered the garden.

"I...I thought I was doing fine," said Maury. "Until I turned around."

"What do you mean?" She still wasn't close enough to see for herself. Still, the evidence was all around me. I was still chewing on the last mouthful.

"It's Shandy," admitted Maury. "I wasn't paying attention to him. When I turned around, I saw that he'd been eating the flowers."

Maury sounded sad. His shoulders drooped as he faced his mother.

She stood silently, studying the damage. "He sure did, didn't he?" she said at last.

"I'm sorry," mumbled Maury. "I just didn't think that he'd eat things."

"Lambs don't belong in gardens," his mother reminded him. "When you do your chores, you'd better leave Shandy in his pen."

Maury shuffled from one foot to another. I knew that he didn't like being separated from me any more than I liked being without him.

"It's good it's just the pansies," said his mother. "He has just nipped them off. Most of them should come back again."

Maury seemed a bit relieved.

"Now, you'd better get him out of here before he has a chance to do more damage."

"C'mon, Shandy," Maury called and started from the garden. "You'll have to stay in your pen for the rest of the day," Maury told me. "You can't be eating up all of our flowers."

I was taken back to the sheep barn and put in my pen. Either I was getting bigger or my pen was getting smaller. I was beginning to hate it. It was much more fun playing outside. Would I have to live in my pen forever?

CHAPTER
Twelve

A few days later, my flower munching seemed to have been forgotten. Maury's mother let him play with me again, and I stayed out of trouble long enough for Maury to think I had learned my lesson.

One afternoon, while Maury and Jenny were playing tag, I wandered over to the edge of the yard. I was curious about a small building off to the side. I'd heard Maury call it the coal bin, and I wanted to see what was inside. If coal tasted anything like the flowers had, I could have a feast!

I entered quietly, ready to run if Maury called me. But he never did. Once my eyes adjusted to the darkness, I could see the coal in piles on the ground.

It didn't taste very good, but it looked like it might be fun to climb. I decided to give it a try.

It *was* fun. I ran up one side and down the other. The black stuff flew all around me, kicking up a cloud of dust.

There was one steep side that I hadn't tried. I decided to see if I could climb it to the top. Backing up, I got a head start and away I ran. Like a mountain sheep, I plunged up the side and toward the top.

I was almost at the top when something began to happen. I felt myself sliding. I scrambled to get my balance, but it was no use. The coal stack was falling, and I was falling with it!

Down we went, sliding toward the floor of the bin. When things finally stopped rolling and the dust settled, I found myself practically buried under the black stuff.

I began to struggle then, but my feet wouldn't move. I was stuck fast in the coal stack.

I was scared. How would I ever get out? I tried to move again, but nothing would give way. I started to cry, trembling with fright.

Maury came running and quickly began to scoop away at the coal with his hands, scolding me as he did so.

"Just look at you," said Maury in exasperation. "You are black from top to bottom. What's Mom gonna say now?"

I looked at Maury. I was really in trouble now.

CHAPTER
Thirteen

Maury led me from the coal bin, all the while keeping a firm hand on my back. Jenny had run to the house to call her mother, and now they were both running across the lawn toward us.

"What in the world happened to you two?" Maury's mother gasped.

"Shandy got into the old coal bin," Maury told her.

"Obviously!" was her comment.

Maury looked down at both of us. We really were quite a mess.

"Well, put him down—back in his own pen. I don't want that mess scattered all over the farm. Then you'll have to wash him

from top to bottom. And when you're through with that, we'll need to talk about where that lamb will be living from now on."

Maury took me back to my pen, all the while talking to me in soothing tones. He and Jenny gathered up a washtub, soap, and water, and they spent a good hour scrubbing the coal out of my wool.

I didn't like it one bit. The soap made me sneeze, and the water was cold. I started to struggle and kick as I bleated out my protest.

"Now, Shandy, be good," Maury scolded. "We've got to clean you up. It's your own fault for going in the coal. I told you to stay out."

"Do you think Mom is going to make Shandy live out in the pasture with the other sheep?" Jenny asked quietly.

Maury gave a big sigh. "I think so. Shandy has been my special friend for a long time now. But he's growing up. The other sheep have been out to pasture for a few days now, and I think Shandy will be happy with them.

So that's where all the sheep have been, I thought to myself. I wondered why it had been so quiet in the barn lately. I was thinking about being out in a pasture when Maury spoke again.

"Shandy isn't a lamb anymore. He's big enough to take care of himself now. I sure will miss him, but I think it's for the best."

I went to bed feeling sad and lonely that night. I couldn't sleep for thinking of Maury's words. Then I cheered up just a bit. Maybe by morning the whole thing would have blown over. Maybe Maury and his family would forget about my trip to the coal bin and just leave me here in my pen.

    That settled, I curled up in my straw and tried to get some sleep.

CHAPTER
Fourteen

I t seems Maury had not forgotten that I was headed out to pasture. Early in the morning, Maury and Jenny came to walk me the short distance to the meadow. I was afraid. Not just to leave Maury, but afraid that once again, the other sheep wouldn't like me.

Maury led me to a large area of grass. The biggest I had ever seen. And all around the grass was a wire fence.

"The fence is to keep the sheep in and other animals out, Shandy," Maury told me. "You'll have all the grass you can eat, and I'll still come out to play with you. But this way you won't get into any more trouble."

I watched as Maury walked back to the open gate, went through, and shut it behind him. Then with a wave of his hand, he was gone.

I looked around. Most of the other sheep were eating grass. A few looked up at me, but no one came over to welcome me or say hi. I took a deep breath and lay down. I was really alone now.

Suddenly, from the other side of the meadow, I heard a terrible sound. A large gray dog had managed to break through the fence. He growled low and mean.

The flock of sheep ran in a group over to the other side of the meadow. In an instant, the dog spotted me. I was all alone, with no way to protect myself. And the dog knew it.

My legs began to tremble. I wanted Maury. I cried as loud as I could, but the dog circled closer.

And then there was a flash of brown fur. There were two dogs in the meadow. But as they were tumbling around, I recognized it was Babs, the sheepdog.

Babs had rescued me! In no time the stray dog had leaped the fence, running away with his tail between his legs.

"Are you all right?" Babs asked me.

I was shaking with fear. I couldn't even answer her.

Then Maury and his father were running toward us. They must have heard Babs' barking.

"Good work, Babs!" cried Maury. "Good job."

It took a while for everyone to settle down again. Maury and his father made sure all the sheep were okay. Then they fixed the fence so that the stray dog couldn't get back in. Once they were finished, they turned to go.

"I don't think you'll have any more problems," Maury's father said to us. "And Babs will always be here to do her job. She'll watch out for you."

Maury came over to me and wrapped his arms around my neck. "See, Shandy? I knew you'd do just fine out here in the pasture. I'm proud of you."

CHAPTER
Fifteen

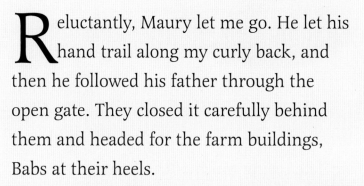

Reluctantly, Maury let me go. He let his hand trail along my curly back, and then he followed his father through the open gate. They closed it carefully behind them and headed for the farm buildings, Babs at their heels.

The flock began to press in closer. I could hear the shuffling and the tramping. As they drew nearer, I could also hear them talking.

"What kind of creature is it, anyway?"

A big ewe stepped forward. "Why, a sheep, dear," she said knowingly.

"A sheep?"

"Of course. A sheep."

"You mean... you mean like us?" someone asked.

The big ewe looked down her nose. "Of course," she said again. "He's one of us."

The big ewe turned to me. She lifted her head and gave me a smile. "I don't think we'll be seeing much of that mean dog again. Thanks to you! You kept him from attacking all of us. We owe our lives to you," she said. Then she added, "Would you like to join our flock?"

Their flock? I was one of them? The truth began to sink in slowly. I was meant to live here. I was a pasture sheep.

I looked about me. They were all there, crowding in around me. The ewes. The lambs. And I was one of them. I would never be alone again—not even when Maury was at school. I had friends and family—lots of them. I was a member of the flock.

With a pleasant smile on my face, I followed the cluster of ewes as they moved back to grazing. Right beside the largest one, I reached down and nipped off a mouthful of sweet meadow grass. No one offered one word of complaint.

Yes sirree! I was going to really enjoy being a sheep.

BETHANY BACKYARD®

PICTURE BOOKS

Spunky's First Christmas
by Janette Oke

Spunky's Camping Adventure
by Janette Oke

Spunky's Circus Adventure
by Janette Oke

Annie Ashcraft Looks Into the Dark
by Ruth Senter

Cows in the House
by Beverly Lewis

Princess Bella and the Red Velvet Hat
by T. Davis Bunn

Making Memories
by Janette Oke

Hold the Boat!
by Jeremiah Gamble

Annika's Secret Wish
by Beverly Lewis

Fifteen Flamingos
by Elspeth Campbell Murphy

Sanji's Seed
by B. J. Reinhard

Happy Easter, God!
by Elspeth Campbell Murphy

BOARD BOOKS
by Christine Tangvald

God Made Colors...For Me!
God Made Shapes...For Me!

God's 123s...For Me!
God's ABCs...For Me!

REBUS PICTURE BOOKS
by Christine Tangvald

The Bible Is...For Me!
Christmas Is...For Me!

Easter Is...For Me!
Jesus Is...For Me!

FIRST CHAPTER BOOKS
by Janette Oke

Spunky's Diary
The Prodigal Cat
The Impatient Turtle
Prairie Dog Town
Maury Had a little Lamb

This Little Pig
New Kid in Town
Ducktails
Trouble in a Fur Coat

NONFICTION

Glow-in-the-Dark Fish and 59 More Ways to See God Through His Creation
by B. J. Reinhard

The Wonderful Way Babies Are Made by Larry Christenson

Fins, Feathers, and Faith by William L. Coleman